**GEO**

P9-AFY-161

# Dear Parent:

Congratulations! Your child is taking the first steps on an exciting journey. The destination? Independent reading!

**STEP INTO READING®** will help your child get there. The program offers books at five levels that accompany children from their first attempts at reading to reading success. Each step includes fun stories, fiction and nonfiction, and colorful art. There are also Step into Reading Sticker Books, Step into Reading Math Readers, and Step into Reading Phonics Readers— a complete literacy program with something to interest every child.

## Learning to Read, Step by Step!

### Ready to Read  Preschool–Kindergarten
• big type and easy words • rhyme and rhythm • picture clues
For children who know the alphabet and are eager to begin reading.

### Reading with Help  Preschool–Grade 1
• basic vocabulary • short sentences • simple stories
For children who recognize familiar words and sound out new words with help.

### Reading on Your Own  Grades 1–3
• engaging characters • easy-to-follow plots • popular topics
For children who are ready to read on their own.

### Reading Paragraphs  Grades 2–3
• challenging vocabulary • short paragraphs • exciting stories
For newly independent readers who read simple sentences with confidence.

### Ready for Chapters  Grades 2–4
• chapters • longer paragraphs • full-color art
For children who want to take the plunge into chapter books but still like colorful pictures.

**STEP INTO READING®** is designed to give every child a successful reading experience. The grade levels are only guides. Children can progress through the steps at their own speed, developing confidence in their reading, no matter what their grade.

Remember, a lifetime love of reading starts with a single step!

For the gallant Sir Robby
—Jane O'Connor

For Tess
—John O'Brien

Text copyright © 2005 by Jane O'Connor. Illustrations copyright © 2005 by John O'Brien.
All rights reserved under International and Pan-American Copyright Conventions. Published
in the United States by Random House Children's Books, a division of Random House, Inc.,
New York, and simultaneously in Canada by Random House of Canada Limited, Toronto.

www.stepintoreading.com

Educators and librarians, for a variety of teaching tools, visit us at
www.randomhouse.com/teachers

*Library of Congress Cataloging-in-Publication Data*
O'Connor, Jane.
Sir Small and the sea monster / by Jane O'Connor ; illustrated by John O'Brien.
    p.  cm. — (Step into reading. Step 2)
SUMMARY: When the prince of Itty Bitty City is stolen by a sea monster, Sir Small sets off to
rescue him.
ISBN 0-375-82565-7 (trade) — ISBN 0-375-92565-1 (lib. bdg.)
[1. Knights and knighthood—Fiction. 2. Sea monsters—Fiction. 3. Size—Fiction.]
I. O'Brien, John, ill. II. Title. III. Series.
PZ7.O222Sk 2005  [E]—dc22  2004002276

Printed in the United States of America  First Edition  10 9 8 7 6 5 4 3 2 1

STEP INTO READING, RANDOM HOUSE, and the Random House colophon are registered trademarks
of Random House, Inc.

# STEP INTO READING®

# Sir Small and the Sea Monster

by Jane O'Connor
illustrated by John O'Brien

Random House 🏠 New York

Long, long ago,
there lived a tiny knight.
His name was Sir Small.

One day, he rode
his trusty ant
into Itty Bitty City.
It was a pretty city.

The castle had towers
as tall as candlesticks.
Every house was
as big and as fancy
as a candy box.

But everybody
was crying!
"What is wrong?"
Sir Small asked.

"A sea monster
has grabbed
our little prince,"
a lady said.

Sir Small looked down
at the sea.
It was as wide and
as deep as a rain puddle.

There was a sea monster!

It had green skin.

It had big, round eyes.

It went

Ga-dunk! GA-DUNK!

"It came from the sky,"
the lady told him.
"It landed with
a big splash.
The little prince
was in a boat.
His boat came back.
But our little prince
did not."

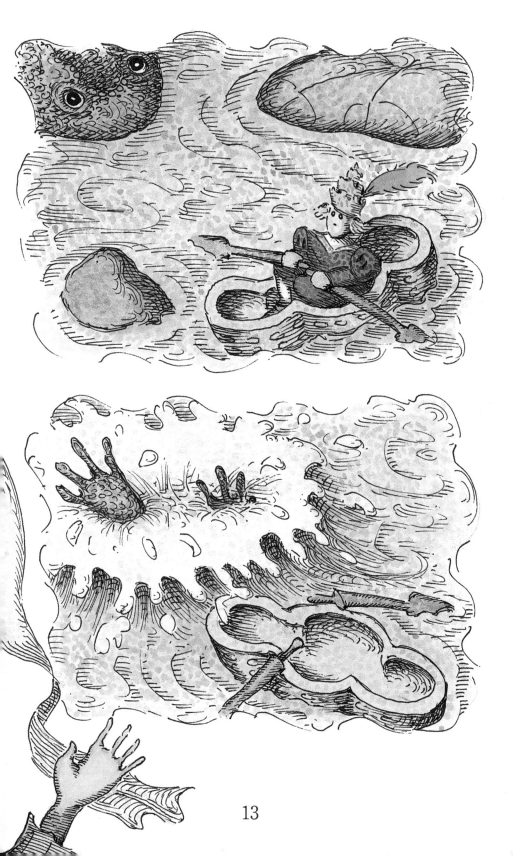

Sir Small ran
inside the castle.
The queen was crying.
So were all the lords
and ladies.
Boo hoo hoo!

"Have no fear.

Sir Small is here,"

he said.

"Sir who?" said the queen.

"You sure are mighty small."

Sir Small held up

his lance.

It was no longer

than a needle.

"I am small.

But I am mighty.

I will fight

the sea monster.

I will save the prince."

Sir Small rode down
to the sea.

He hopped

on a royal sea horse.

He rode right up
to the sea monster.
"Go away!"
shouted Sir Small.

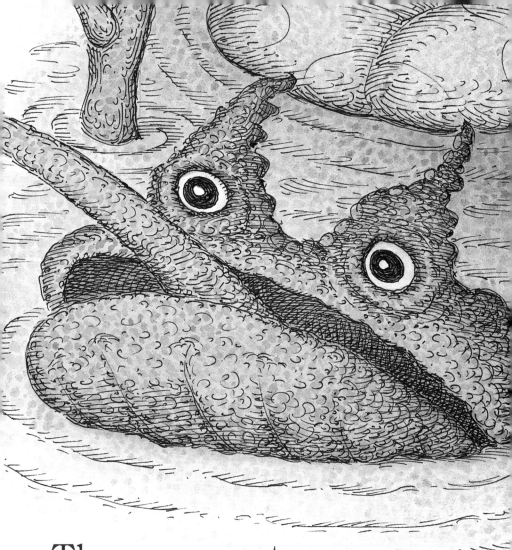

The sea monster
did not go away.

It opened its wide mouth.

It stuck out its tongue.

"That is very rude!"
said Sir Small.
He poked the
sea monster
with his lance.

That did it!

Up leaped the sea monster.

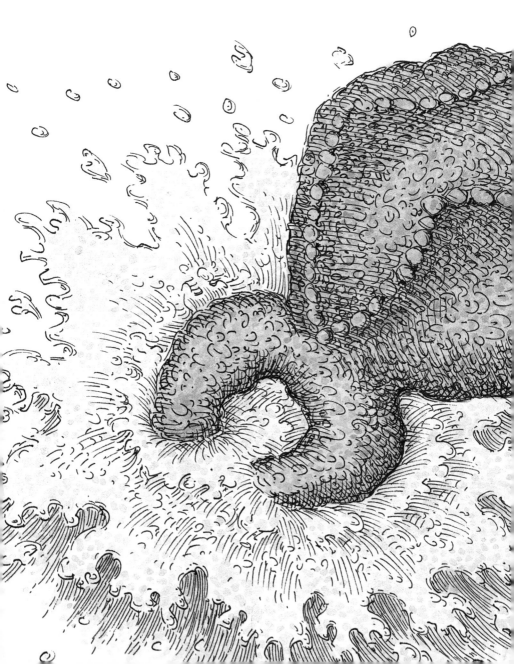

Down it landed.

THUD!

Then the sea monster
hop hop hopped away.

But where was
the little prince?
Had the sea monster
eaten him?

No!

He was hiding

in a snail shell.

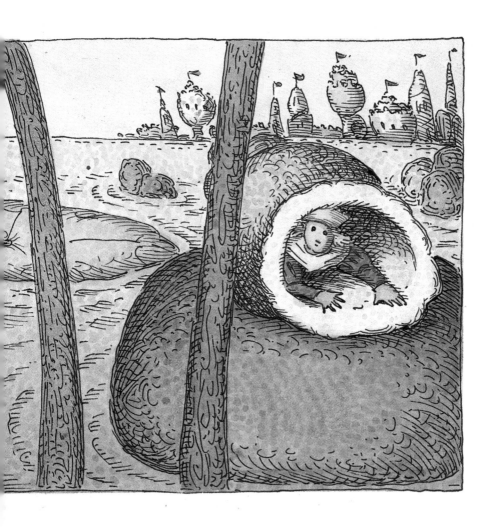

# "Hop on,"
# said Sir Small.

Away they rode
on the sea horse.

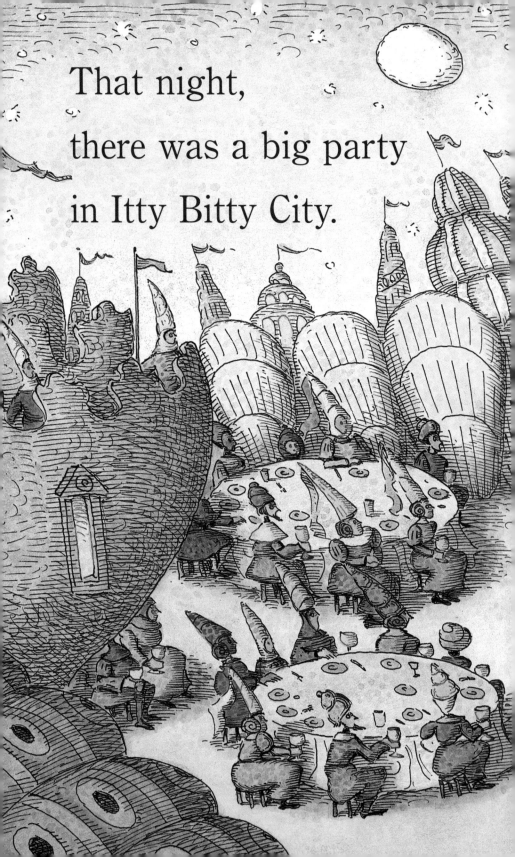

That night,
there was a big party
in Itty Bitty City.

The little prince sat
next to Sir Small.

The queen stood up.

She said,

"Here's to Sir Small—

the smallest

and bravest of all."